Victoria Turnbull

Cloud Forest

Frances Lincoln
Children's Books

For Jo, my sister

Brimming with creative inspiration, how-to projects, and useful information to enrich your everyday life, Quarto Knows is a favourite destination for those pursuing their interests and passions. Visit our site and dig deeper with our books into your area of interest: Quarto Creates, Quarto Cooks, Quarto Homes, Quarto Lives, Quarto Drives, Quarto Explores, Quarto Gifts, or Quarto Kids.

Text and illustrations © Victoria Turnbull 2019.
First published in 2019 by Frances Lincoln Children's Books.
First published in paperback in 2020 by Frances Lincoln Children's Books, an imprint of The Quarto Group.
The Old Brewery, 6 Blundell Street, London N7 9BH, United Kingdom.
T (0)20 7700 6700 F (0)20 7700 8066 www.QuartoKnows.com

A catalogue record for this book is available from the British Library.
ISBN 978-0-7112-5194-6
The illustrations were created with graphite and coloured pencil
Set in Bellota
Published by Katie Cotton
Designed by Zoë Tucker
Edited by Katie Cotton
Production by Caragh McAleenan
Manufactured in Guangdong, China TT022020

1 3 5 7 9 8 6 4 2

MIX
Paper from responsible sources
FSC® C016973
www.fsc.org

Umpa's garden was filled
with flowers and fruit trees.
It was my favourite place.

Sometimes Umpa forgot to water the garden.
But the clouds remembered for him.

He showed me how to poke
the little seeds into the warm earth
with my fingers and we waited
for them to grow.

A story will help,

Umpa said.

Stories make everything grow.

So he read to me
and I learned to
follow the words...

Through the garden gate,

over the treetops,

across the meadow...

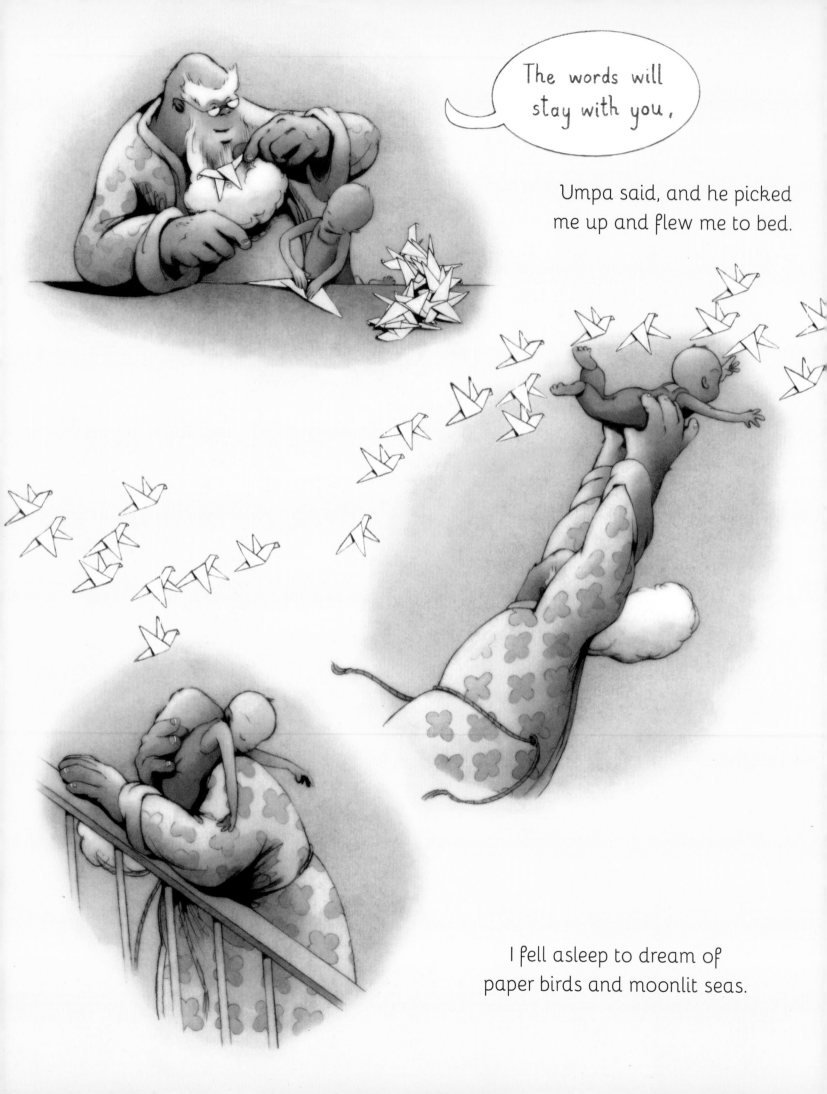

The words will stay with you,

Umpa said, and he picked me up and flew me to bed.

I fell asleep to dream of paper birds and moonlit seas.

That night the seeds began to grow.

As the first green shoots poked up through the earth,
we followed the words in search of castles in the sky.

When the rains came and
an ocean spilled from above,
Umpa gathered us up and
we sailed away to keep
our feet dry.

After the rains,
the sky was huge with stars.
The words sheltered us from monsters
that crept from the dark.

By Umpa's birthday,
the garden was in full bloom.
We feasted with friends until
the day was done.

The words made
our wishes come true.

Then Umpa was gone,
and he didn't come back.
For a time I hated
everything.

I no longer searched for
castles in the sky. Or dreamed of
paper birds and moonlit seas.
And I couldn't see the stars.
The clouds had swallowed
me whole.

Until one day,
I remembered what
Umpa had
left me.

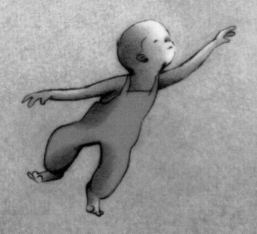

A path of words to follow...

which always leads me back,

to him.